BINGO BROWN'S GUIDE TO ROMANCE

Bingo found that he was badly shaken and short of breath. The shock of thinking he had seen Melissa was as great as if he had seen Melissa.

There was a convex mirror at the end of the aisle. . . . In this mirror he had a good look at the girl who looked exactly like Melissa, and he found that it was Melissa.

No other girl had that hair, those eyes. No other girl had that T-shirt with the Declaration of Independence on it.

Bingo had only seen that T-shirt one other time—on the day of the T-shirt wear-in—but he had never forgotten it. It had been her mom's shirt and was very, very large on her. Now, however, the shirt was not so large. Either the shirt had shrunk or Melissa had enlarged.

He checked the mirror.

The shirt had not shrunk.

Therefore Melissa had enlarged.

Bingo Brown's
Guide to Romance

PUFFIN BOOKS BY BETSY BYARS

After the Goat Man
An ALA Notable Book

Bingo Brown and the Language of Love

Bingo Brown, Gypsy Lover

The Burning Questions of Bingo Brown

The Cartoonist

The Computer Nut

Cracker Jackson
An ALA Notable Book

The Cybil War
An ALA Notable Book

The 18th Emergency

The Glory Girl

The House of Wings
An ALA Notable Book

The Midnight Fox

The Summer of the Swans
Winner of the Newbery Medal

Trouble River
An ALA Notable Book

The TV Kid

BETSY BYARS

Bingo Brown's
Guide to Romance

PUFFIN BOOKS

PUFFIN BOOKS
Published by the Penguin Group
Penguin Books USA Inc., 375 Hudson Street, New York, New York 10014, U.S.A.
Penguin Books Ltd, 27 Wrights Lane, London W8 5TZ, England
Penguin Books Australia Ltd, Ringwood, Victoria, Australia
Penguin Books Canada Ltd, 10 Alcorn Avenue, Toronto, Ontario, Canada M4V 3B2
Penguin Books (N.Z.) Ltd, 182-190 Wairau Road, Auckland 10, New Zealand

Penguin Books Ltd, Registered Offices: Harmondsworth, Middlesex, England

First published in the United States of America by Viking Penguin,
a division of Penguin Books USA Inc., 1992
Published in Puffin Books, 1994

1 3 5 7 9 10 8 6 4 2

THE LIBRARY OF CONGRESS HAS CATALOGED THE VIKING PENGUIN EDITION AS FOLLOWS:
Byars, Betsy Cromer
Bingo Brown's guide to romance / by Betsy Byars.   p.   cm.
Summary: Bingo Brown's work on his definitive "Guide to Romance"
hits a snag when his long-distance girlfriend Melissa
returns unexpectedly from Oklahoma.
ISBN 0-670-84491-8
I. Title   PZ7.B9836Bif   1992   [Fic]—dc20   91-42266   CIP   AC

Puffin Books ISBN 0-14-036080-8

Printed in the United States of America
Set in Sabon

Contents

Bingo's Challenge

Bingo Brown had told his mom that he was bored and needed new challenges, and he was now on his way to the laundromat to wash the family's clothes.

All his protests had been in vain.

"By new challenges, I didn't mean wash clothes, Mom," he had said, at first trying to be patient. His father had warned him, correctly, that women with new babies were sometimes easily irritated.

"Well, you've never washed clothes before, have you?"

"No."

"Then it will be a new challenge."

"Mom, the laundromat is right next door to Columbo's, and my friends hang out there, eating pizza and playing video games and—"

"Wash the baby's things separately and divide the rest of the clothes into piles, bright colors in one, whites and pastels in another."

"Why don't we just wait until the washer is fixed?" Bingo went on with reason and good humor. "I could run to K Mart and get us some underwear and Jamie some disposable diapers and—"

"If I had wanted you to run to K Mart and get underwear, I would have asked you to go to K Mart and get underwear."

Her nostrils flared, which was not a good sign. "I'm working tomorrow and I can't leave the babysitter with all these dirty clothes. Look, if you don't want to go to the laundromat, just say, 'I don't want to go to the laundromat.'"

"Thanks." With a shrug of regret, he repeated, "I don't want to go to the laundromat."

"Fine! Great!" Her nostrils were so flared now that Bingo thought he caught sight of her brain. "Then go to your room for the rest of your life."

Faced with those two choices, Bingo manfully picked up the basket of dirty clothes.

Now he was on his bicycle, pedaling to the King Koin Laundromat. He had a bushel basket of dirty clothes strapped on the back of the bicycle, and he had to take the long way to the laundromat so none of his friends would see his unfortunate burden.

To pass the time, he began working on his *Guide to Romance, A Record of the Personal Ups and Downs of Bingo Brown. Dedicated to My Brother, Jamie, as a Guide and Comfort to Him When He Finds Himself, as He Surely Will, upon the Roller Coaster of Life.*

Bingo was now working on the section that contained romantic problems with their solutions. Bingo was determined not to spare himself, even though many of the problems were extremely personal.

> *Problem #1. The Xeroxed Love Letter.*
> Suppose that you have written a love letter and suppose that this love letter turns out to be the best love letter in the history of the world and suppose you want to save this letter for future generations and with this in mind, you make a Xerox of the letter and in your haste to mail the letter, you mail the Xerox of the letter. Will this take away from the warmth of the words?
>
> *Bingo's Answer:* Yes, for I myself have been waiting for three long months for an answer to just such a Xeroxed letter.

Bingo broke off his thoughts and cut swiftly around the back of Winn Dixie, past the dumpsters, and behind Rexall Drugs, and peered around the corner of Columbo's Pizza. Seeing no one he knew, he pedaled quickly to the

King Koin. He rode through the open doors and came to a screeching halt at the first available washing machine.

He could not be bothered with patiently separating the clothes. If any of his friends were on their way to Columbo's to spend a pleasant hour with the video games, just as he would like to do, and saw him with little prissy piles of clothes—pink over here, blue over here, pink with blue flowers over here . . . The thought caused Bingo to shudder.

There were too many clothes for one washer, so Bingo crammed what he could in one washer, crammed the rest in the next washer. Still too many, so he put the remaining diapers into a third washer and slammed down the lids. His heart was pounding.

He made quick work of the change machine and soon the machines were rumbling happily. Bingo went outside for some badly needed fresh air.

While he was standing there, fanning himself with a box of Rinso, he found himself thinking about life—about how in the old days when a boy asked his mom for a new challenge, she sent him to the Crusades or out West to look for gold or on a whaling ship bound for northern climes or—

"Hey, Worm Brain." A voice broke harshly into his thoughts.

Bingo saw with displeasure that Billy Wentworth was standing in front of him. He sighed. "What do you want, Wentworth?"

Wentworth was chewing gum and he paused to blow a small purple bubble about the size of a Ping-Pong ball. That done, he said, "I just saw that girl."

"What girl?"

"The girl that used to be in our room. The one you used to like."

Bingo's heart began to thud against the Rinso box, which he had wrapped in both arms. Actually there had been many girls in Bingo's life—the future President of the United States, the would-be orchestra conductor, Cici, Boots—but his only true love had been Dr. Jekyll and Ms. Hyde, known to everyone else as Melissa.

Obviously Wentworth couldn't know that, because Melissa was miles away in Bixby, Oklahoma. Still, the thought of her was enough to make Bingo's imprisoned heart attempt to burst right out of his chest, through the box of Rinso, and fly nonstop to Bixby.

This—Bingo knew—was why chests were made so strong. Ribs were designed for one thing. They were prison bars to keep hearts from doing anything foolish. Bingo had been grateful for ribs many times in his life, and particularly now.

Bingo said in a controlled voice, "What girl would that be, Wentworth?"

"Melissa."

Bingo dropped the Rinso box with a thud.

"M-Melissa."

"Yeah, M-Melissa."

"But Melissa's in Oklahoma."

Wentworth paused long enough to create another purple bubble. "No, she's not. She's in Winn Dixie."

"W-Winn Dixie?"

"Yes, W-Winn Dixie."

"But she couldn't be. She's in Bixby, Oklahoma."

"Not anymore."

"I don't believe you."

"So . . . check it out."

Bingo turned at once toward the grocery store and then stopped. Wentworth would enjoy seeing him rush into the store like a heartsick fool.

"Where, exactly, was she in the store?"

"She and this other girl had gotten a cart with a bad wheel, and they were trying to get it through Produce."

"What makes you think the girl was Melissa?"

"I got eyes."

Still Bingo hesitated.

"Look," Wentworth said, "you don't believe me, check it out."

"That's what I intend to do."

"Be my guest." Wentworth pulled down his camouflage T-shirt in a forceful manner.

Bingo's heart was pounding so hard it was as if tom-tom drums were being beaten inside the grocery store, deafening him.

"Hey, Worm Brain."

Bingo heard that. He turned.

"You forgot your R-Rinso!"

Bingo returned to the Rinso box and the small pile of blue flakes that had leaked out. It was amazing, the amount of dignity required to pick up a box of Rinso with Wentworth sneering. Bingo felt he did as well as anyone could.

He even managed to say thanks without stuttering.

Then he headed manfully for whatever awaited him amid the groceries.

Through the Sliding Doors

Bingo approached the sliding doors of Winn Dixie with caution, but they flew open anyway. Bingo stepped back quickly. Two shoppers passed him with curious looks, but Bingo remained against the side of the building.

When the doors had once again shut, Bingo moved forward. Without touching the floor mats, he peered inside.

Bingo had recently been fitted for glasses. He had wanted glasses for years—not because he couldn't see well, but because he liked the idea of himself in glasses. He was the type for glasses.

Finally he had convinced his parents of his need, and now—the very moment when he really needed glasses to see into the depths of Winn Dixie—they were still at the eye doctor's, being ground to prescription.

Even without his glasses, he could see that Melissa was not in sight.

Bingo was tempted to turn around immediately, retrieve the family's laundry, and mark the whole thing up to a cruel trick of Wentworth's. Certainly Wentworth was capable of that sort of cruelty, but Wentworth wasn't sensitive enough to sense the depth of Bingo's longing for Melissa and take advantage of it.

Bingo cracked his knuckles in a manly fashion. He would have spit on his hands but they were already wet with sweat. Bingo prided himself on his manly gestures and hoped, sometime in the future, to get the mature feelings that went along with them.

"You going in, Worm Brain, you gotta open the doors, like this."

Wentworth stepped around Bingo onto the mat, and the doors opened. Without looking at Wentworth, Bingo entered.

He took a cart—he hadn't intended to do that, and behind him Wentworth gave a snort of disgust. Bingo put his box of Rinso in the baby's seat and set off. The cart wanted to turn immediately into a display of paper towels, but Bingo wrestled it to Produce.

Bingo moved slowly through Produce. He watched the mirrors at the end of the fruit-and-vegetable aisle to see if Billy Wentworth had followed him into the store.

Bingo seemed to be in everyone's way, so he muttered

beneath his breath, "Grapefruit ... lettuce ... kum-
quats ... we have those ... celery ... parsnips ... not
quite fresh enough ..."

This took him to the bakery department.

He went quickly past the loaves of bread and brought
his cart to an abrupt stop. He peered around a pyramid
of macaroni-and-cheese dinners. Billy Wentworth was still
outside the store. Now he could devote his full attention
to finding Melissa.

He proceeded more slowly now, giving each aisle the
caution a hunter would give the jungle. He did not think
Melissa would be in Baby Supplies and, of course, she
wasn't, but he paused there to put a box of disposable
diapers in his cart. That, he thought, gave him the look of
a serious shopper. If he did run into Melissa, that would
make a good impression.

He continued. Of course she would not be in Pet Products, but he gave that aisle the same caution as the others.

He was gaining in confidence now. There were only
two aisles left—Soft Drinks and Health Supplies.

By now, Bingo thought he knew what had happened.
Wentworth had seen someone who looked like Melissa—
after all, there were other girls with incredibly beautiful,
beribboned hair and jazzy lips, girls whose eyes had a little
squint that would make a man's heart beat faster.

Wentworth might even have said, "Hi, Melissa," and
the girl hadn't bothered to say, "I'm not Melissa," and this
had reinforced the mistaken identification. Therefore

Wentworth genuinely believed he had seen the real Melissa and reported it as the truth.

This explanation made Bingo feel better. Melissa was still safely in Bixby, Oklahoma.

And, Bingo went on as his spirits began to lift, this would give him an excuse to write an amusing letter. "Today, I almost saw you in the grocery store. Billy Wentworth thought he saw you, and I, of course, rushed into the store and . . ."

And he definitely would not Xerox the letter when he finished—no matter how perfect it was!

The soft drink aisle was empty, and Bingo pushed his cart directly into Health Supplies. One of the cart wheels stuck, and Bingo came to an abrupt halt. He glanced down and saw the trouble. A leaf of lettuce was jammed into the wheel.

He knelt, dislodged the leaf of lettuce, and looked up.

There she was!

Melissa was in Health Supplies!

Melissa and a friend were picking out a box of health supplies!

Fortunately Bingo was on his knees, so he was able to duck-walk backwards, pulling the cart with him, into the safety of Soft Drinks.

Here, after a few tense moments, he was able to straighten up.

Melissa—if it was Melissa—had been reading the directions on a box, and her head had been bent—so maybe it wasn't Melissa at all. Maybe it was a girl so like Melissa that he had made the same mistake as Billy Wentworth.

Bingo found that he was badly shaken and short of breath. The shock of thinking he had seen Melissa was as great as if he had seen Melissa. He was glad for the support of the grocery cart.

There was a convex mirror at the end of the aisle to keep people from stealing health supplies. Bingo had read only this week that the most frequently stolen product was Preparation H, so this mirror was a must.

In this mirror he had a good look at the girl who looked exactly like Melissa, and he found that it was Melissa.

No other girl had that hair, those eyes. No other girl had that T-shirt with the Declaration of Independence on it.

Bingo had only seen that T-shirt one other time, on the day of the T-shirt wear-in, but he had never forgotten it. It had been her mom's shirt and was very, very large on her. Now, however, the shirt was not so large. Either the shirt had shrunk or Melissa had enlarged.

He checked the mirror.

The shirt had not shrunk.

Therefore Melissa had enlarged.

He checked again.

The phrase "bigger than life" came to his mind and stayed there. Melissa was bigger than life.

He had a brief but troubling picture of her seeing him and holding out her arms. He would hold out his arms, too, of course, anything else would be unthinkable, but—and this is where the picture got troubling—when they met, where would their arms go? He knew where the arms went if the boy was taller, but now he was shorter.

Bingo's arms began to twitch nervously, as if they wanted to reach out and hold back at the same time. He understood his arms' reluctance. If his arms misjudged her size and reached out too low or too high, it might be embarrassing. Well, perhaps if one arm reached high and the other low, they could sort of meet around her without actually touching anything. That is, unless she reached out low-high, too, and her high arm hit his high arm and her low—

He forced himself to look at the situation rationally.

Problem #2. Girl Larger than Usual.

Suppose that you have not seen a girl for a long, long time. And the last time you saw this girl was on the front porch of her house. Suppose that even though her mother was watching, you kissed her good-bye because she was moving to a place like Bixby, Oklahoma, and you might never have this opportunity again. And so you leaned down—because she was smaller than you—and kissed her. Suppose months pass, and the next time you see this girl she has grown enough so that you will no longer be the one who has to bend down for the kiss. Should this deter you?

Bingo's Answer: No, but other things might deter you, like the fact that she didn't answer your letter or let you know she was coming to town and was more interested in securing health supplies than in seeing you. Those things are far, far more important than height, which is—after all—only a statistic.

Bingo had now worked out the situation to his satisfaction, and he pushed his cart boldly into Health Supplies.

Melissa was gone.

Melissa's Clone

"Excuse me."

"What?"

"I'd like to get by, please." It was a woman with a grocery cart.

"Of course," Bingo said.

He discovered he was still blocking the aisle of health supplies. He pushed his cart quickly against the deodorants.

As Bingo waited for the lady to pass he checked the convex mirror. He didn't see Melissa, as he had hoped. He saw something he had hoped not to see—Billy Wentworth.

Wentworth was in the meat department, moving as if by radar straight to Health Supplies. Bingo U-turned his cart and moved to the front of the store.

Again no Melissa, but he sensed Wentworth was now moving to the front of the store, too.

Bingo abandoned his cart and began darting through the aisles, looking for Melissa. He had to see her again. He had to.

And he had to do this without Wentworth witnessing the meeting. He needed time to get his arms under control, to say nothing of his face, his thoughts, and the rest of himself. He stopped.

Melissa was at the end of Pet Products. Bingo rushed down the aisle and stopped behind a pyramid of Kibbles 'n Bits.

Melissa and her friend passed directly in front of him—not five feet away—on their way to the checkout counters.

The girl with Melissa glanced in his direction—the pyramid wasn't high enough to hide him completely—and she said something to Melissa. Bingo waited with his heart in his throat for Melissa to turn, to meet his eyes, to speak.

But Melissa did none of those things. She was concentrating on getting a place in the express lane.

Melissa was saying, "I can give the best home perms of anybody. My mom says I could be a beautician. This— my hair—"

She shook her head, and her hair flew out with such vigor Bingo could feel the breeze from it against his pale face.

Her earrings jangled. And these were not the tasteful

gypsy earrings Bingo had given her last Christmas. These earrings were as big as handcuffs.

"—this is a home perm, but I don't broadcast the fact. Most people think it's natural."

"It sure looks natural."

Melissa turned the box over and checked the instructions. "Do you want body, waves, or curls?" She glanced sideways at her friend, but Bingo thought she looked beyond to where he stood behind Kibbles 'n Bits.

"What do you have?"

"Can't you tell? Curls, obviously."

"I want curls, too."

This exchange caused Bingo's doubts to return. Melissa—his Melissa—had naturally curly hair, didn't she? He had seen it up close. Maybe there was some mousse involved, but . . .

And! This Melissa didn't sound like his Melissa. She sounded like somebody from out of state. It could be something she had picked up in Oklahoma, but Bingo didn't know what an Oklahoman sounded like.

Bingo thought he had caught the faint scent of gingersnaps as she fluffed out her hair, however, and if so, then it was Melissa. No other girl smelled like gingersnaps.

Bingo didn't know what to believe. Burning questions rose as bitter as indigestion.

Was it Melissa or a Melissa clone? Would Melissa come to town to buy health supplies without telling him? Could one girl have gotten that big in a year? Had he gotten bigger, too? And if he had gotten bigger, then how had she gotten even bigger? And—

"Yo, Melissa!"

It was Wentworth.

Melissa turned. "Oh, hi."

"Remember that kid who used to be in our room at school?" Wentworth asked.

"Which one?"

"Named Bingo . . . had a lot of freckles?"

"Yes, I remember."

"Well, he came in the store looking for you."

"Did he? Well, he didn't find me." She smiled.

Bingo's heart leapt in his chest. It was Melissa. Those were her teeth, and no matter how the rest of her had grown, her teeth had remained blessedly the same.

"I'll check around if you want to see him," Wentworth offered.

Bingo got ready to step out.

"Don't bother."

Bingo found that he had already stepped out, but no one noticed. Melissa and her friend went through the checkout line and left the store. Wentworth followed.

Bingo had to follow. He didn't want to. He had to. Then he remembered his mom's box of Rinso.

As if he were being fast-forwarded, he made his way back to Health Supplies, got the Rinso, and returned to the express register.

He gasped to the checkout girl, "I brought this box of soap into the store. See, I thought a girl I knew was in here and since I hadn't seen the girl in a while—her name is Melissa—I was in a hurry to see her and I rushed in and I had just been to the laundromat, which is why I have this half-empty box of soap. Do you need to call security?"

"Not really."

"Thank you."

She waved him on with a bored shrug.

Bingo rushed out into the parking lot, but Melissa and her friend were not in sight. Neither was Wentworth. Bingo stood for a moment clutching his box of Rinso.

He knew he didn't have a moment to waste. He had to get his bike and immediately set out after them.

He spun around, trying to remember where he had left his bicycle.

Then he remembered the laundry. He gave a cry of anguish. If he didn't start after Melissa immediately, he would be a troubled person for the rest of his life, always wondering why Melissa had come to town to buy health supplies, always dangling, suspended in the atmosphere of life, never able to get his feet on the ground.

He saw this as the crossroads of life. If he took the road that led to Melissa, he would find the answer to life's questions and happiness. If he took the road that led to the laundromat, he would find wet clothes.

Bingo sighed.

Slowly, painfully, he made his way to the King Koin. The only thing he had to be grateful for was that Wentworth had not waited to jeer at him.

In the laundromat, he emptied the first washing machines he came to and put the clumps of wet clothes into the basket on his bicycle. Then he pedaled through the doors.

He found himself pedaling faster as he crossed the parking lot.

Maybe all was not lost. Maybe there was still a chance. He could ride up Main Street and, if she wasn't there, take an immediate left onto Madison.

He pedaled harder, bending over his handlebars, and then he stiffened. He braked so fast he left rubber on the sidewalk.

He didn't want to see Melissa now. And he certainly didn't want Melissa to see him.

Problem #3. Sustaining Romance.

Suppose that you are forced, by family reversals, to carry a load of wet laundry on the back of your bicycle. And suppose that in the past you have presented yourself as a knowing, cool, gypsy-type lover. Will the sight of you with a load of unattractive wet laundry dampen this romantic picture as well as the flame of passion in her heart, or will

it bring out her maternal instincts and a new depth
to the flagging relationship previously . . .

Bingo didn't bother to answer the question.

Once again, he took the long, painfully slow route
home.

Love Letters for Eternity

Dear Melissa,

Bingo was at home. He sat at his desk, hunched over the much-creased sheet of notebook paper.

His hands appeared to be steady, but the paper trembled, as if it had somehow absorbed the shock of the event in Health Supplies.

Dear Melissa,

Bingo tried to remember when he had written those two words—it had been at least three months ago, but he remembered the moment as clearly as if it had occurred yesterday.

He had started the letter, thinking it was going to be just one of his usual outstanding letters, and then—and then the pen had begun to move across the paper on its own, as if by magic, and that was when Bingo had realized this was going to be a love letter for eternity, maybe even infinity.

Bingo glanced back at his bed because he felt the need to lie down, but his bed was unmade. Not only that, but his mother had replaced his Smurf sheets with Teenage Mutant Ninja Turtles, which had been on sale.

Bingo could barely sleep on the turtles, much less read a love letter for eternity on them.

He glanced at his letter and read what he had written:

Dear Melissa,

He looked up at the ceiling.

There was no need to continue reading the letter because he knew it by heart. The letter was that perfect.

It was too perfect. Actually, how he wished it hadn't been quite so perfect because then he wouldn't have Xeroxed it.

> *I have been thinking of you since breakfast. We only had Corn Pops because the baby had cried all night, and at first I thought my unsettled feeling had to do with an unsatisfactory breakfast.*

Then came the sentence that had told Bingo that this was going to be a letter for eternity.

> *At nine-thirty I pedaled to Wendy's for a sausage biscuit, and after I ate a sausage biscuit and fries,*

*I was still hungry. Then I realized that my hunger
was for you.*

*The hunger of love, and this is truly the first
time I have experienced it so intensely, is a unique
experience, Melissa, and I sat in Wendy's until the
waitress wiped my table three times and gave me
a funny look. Then I went home and had a small
box of Cheerios and felt a little better.*

The letter went on in that heated manner for a full
page. He had sent the letter off and waited anxiously for
her reply. It wasn't like Melissa not to answer immediately.
For a letter like this, she should have called.

And what a phone call it would have been!

Her voice would have undergone that wonderful
change, deepening with pleasure as she thanked him. Girls
were fortunate to be able to deepen their voices so attrac-
tively, and a thank-you in a voice deep with pleasure was
something a man could carry in his heart forever.

At that time he had not, of course, been aware that
he had sent the Xerox of the letter, or that she would be
offended by it.

He looked down and his eyes took in the letter's
closing.

Hungrily yours,
Bingo

There was a knock on his window.

"I'm busy, Wentworth," he called without turning his head.

"Did I lie?"

Bingo decided to play it cool. "About what?"

"About that girl."

"What girl?"

"Melissa."

"Yes. Yes, I saw her."

"Then did I lie?"

"No, Wentworth. Not this time."

"And I know something else about Melissa—but it'll cost you."

From the living room his mom's voice cut into his conversation. "Bingo!"

"I'm busy," he called back.

If only everyone would leave him alone while he was in anguish. He couldn't concentrate on his anguish while people kept interrupting. There was no respect for anguish anymore.

"Bingo!"

His mother was in the doorway now. She stood with the basket of wet clothes on her hip.

Bingo did not want to have another conversation with his mother like the one he had just had. He had come in from the laundromat hot and flushed, as stunned as if life had hit him over the head with a baseball bat. And his mother had unfeelingly said—no, his mother had snapped—"Where's the laundry?"

"Oh, it's still on my bicycle, I guess. Mom, the most terrible thing in the world happened!"

"Well, bring in the clothes so I can dry them. Jamie is in his last clean diaper, aren't you, snookums?"

Jamie, on her shoulder, had begun to drool with excitement. He always did this whenever he saw Bingo because Bingo bounced him up and down better than anybody. Bingo didn't have time to bounce him.

"Mom! Mom, didn't you hear me? The most terrible thing in the world has happened."

His mother had put one hand protectively on the baby. "What?"

"Melissa's back."

"Melissa?"

"Yes, Mom, Melissa—at least I think it was Melissa. It was her shirt and teeth—I know that much."

"Melissa from Oklahoma?"

"Yes!"

"Well, what's terrible about that?"

"Mom!"

"Now you can save money on all those long-distance calls. I should think you'd be delighted to have Melissa back in town."

"Mom!"

"Bring the laundry in and we can discuss it."

"Mom!"

"Now."

So he had brought the laundry in, but by then she had started playing with the baby.

"Look, Bingo, he can almost stand alone."

"Mom, here are the clothes. Do you want to discuss Melissa now?"

"In a minute. Oh, look, he's standing alone he's standing alone he's standing alone—oh, how long did he keep his balance? It was at least a minute, wasn't it, Bingo?"

"I didn't time it."

"I've got to write that in his baby book. 'Stood alone for one whole minute.' You are the most wonderful baby in the world, yes, you are. You're probably going to be in the Olympics."

Now, his mother was apparently feeling guilty—and rightly so—about her lack of interest. She had come to his room to make up. Now she would want to hear about Melissa—every single detail, only now he did not care to talk about it.

Bingo gave her an aloof look. He was determined not to tell her one single detail of the trauma in Health Supplies, no matter how much she begged.

"Mom, I would like to be alone. Certainly I no longer want to discuss my meeting with Melissa, which was not so much a meeting as a sighting. That's all I can say. I am—I don't know how to explain it—sort of caught on the roller coaster of life, and I don't know if I will ever get off."

"Well, you better get off your roller coaster, and quick."

She shifted the basket of laundry from one hip to the other. And her next words did indeed bring the roller coaster of life to a screeching halt.

"These are not our clothes."

Following Melissa

"I hope for your sake," Bingo's mother said over her shoulder, "that no one has made off with our laundry."

"I hope so, too," Bingo said.

He was sitting in the backseat of the car between the car seat containing Jamie and the basket containing a stranger's load of wash. He was concentrating on making his mind a blank, because there was not one single thought in the entire world that would not bring him discomfort.

His mother kept interrupting the process with a list of the valuable garments in the missing laundry.

"You are aware," she continued, "that all of Jamie's diapers were in those loads."

"I am aware. You told me."

"As well as your father's underwear."

"I know."

"And your father hates new underwear."

"Mom, no one is going to make off with Dad's old underwear."

"Well, you made off with somebody's old sheets."

"I was upset, Mom. I had just had the shock of my life."

Bingo turned to Jamie, who was playing with a set of plastic car keys, shaking them so enthusiastically Jamie had to blink his eyes for fear of being struck in the face.

"So you said. I've had a shock myself today, but I am managing to go on in a reasonably intelligent way."

Bingo looked at his mom. "What kind of shock? Mom, you aren't going to have another baby?"

"Not that big a shock."

"Good. Does it have to do with work?"

She shook her head.

"Me? Is it something I've done?" Bingo broke off before she answered. "Mom!"

"What?"

"There she is! Mom!"

"What? Who?"

"There! See those two girls?"

"Yes."

"Well, the tall one's Melissa."

"Want me to honk?"

"No! No! Whatever you do, don't honk!"

Bingo ducked out of sight because his mother's favorite part of the car was the horn, and she didn't just go *honk*, like that. She went *honk-honk-honk-hooooonk*.

He was not ready to have attention called to himself in that manner. He could not bear to have Melissa's first glimpse of him in a year be of him riding in the backseat of a car with a baby and strange laundry. It was as bad as having her glimpse his face on top of a pyramid of dog food.

"Go around the block, Mom, please."

"What for?"

"Mom, I've got to see where Melissa and her friend go. I've got to!"

"Well, you can't see anything crouched down on the floor of the car."

"I'm not crouched on the floor of the car, Mom. Give me a break."

"I won't go around the block. That takes too long."

"Mom!"

"But I will pull into Wendy's parking lot and wait until they pass by."

"Oh, all right. Mom, thanks."

"I don't know why I'm doing this. If our clothes aren't already stolen, they will be by the time we . . ."

Her voice trailed off as she parked and cut off the engine. There was a silence.

"What's happening?" Bingo asked.

"Nothing. Oh, I'll announce it—like on football. They're coming by. The tall one—are you sure that's Melissa?"

"Yes."

"The tall one is reading something off a box. I'll roll down the window—wait, I'll get out of the car and open up the trunk, like I'm checking the spare tire. That way I can hear exactly what they're saying."

"Don't get out of the car!"

"Oh, all right." She paused to listen. "They're talking about a home permanent."

"They can't still be talking about that. They were talking about that in the store an hour ago."

"Be quiet so I can hear."

"I don't want you to hear. Mom, I just want to know where they go."

"Melissa just said something funny, and one of them sort of snorted like a horse."

"It wasn't Melissa. Melissa doesn't snort."

"I hope not."

"Are they gone? Can I look?"

"No, they stopped. Wait! The short girl is looking across the street because there are two boys there. At last, some action. Apparently she knows the boys and wants to cross the street. But—here's some good news—Melissa does not want to cross the street and pulls her back."

"Mom, are you making this up?"

"No. If I were going to make something up, it would be a lot more interesting."

There was a pause, and then his mother said, "That's it. They've gone. You can get up now."

Bingo raised his head. He could see the back of Melissa's Declaration of Independence T-shirt as she and her friend moved out of sight.

"So are you satisfied? Can we go retrieve our clothes?"

"No, Mom, no! I've got to see where they're going. That's the whole point of this."

"Surely you don't expect me to follow Melissa all over town."

"Mom, I won't ever be able to find her! Maybe she'll go back to Bixby and I'll never see her at all. And . . . and I'm almost ready to face her now."

"If you're so crazy to face her, get out of the car, catch up with her."

"Mom, please!"

"I'll make a deal with you."

"Mom, this is no time for deals. Melissa is walking out of my life forever!"

"Here is the deal. We go to the laundromat. You get our clothes. And if, *if* they're all there, we'll come back and follow Melissa."

"She'll be gone by then! Mom, please!"

Bingo's mother drove out of the parking lot. "Get down on the floor, we're passing them," she said.

Bingo ducked just as his mother sounded the horn. "Mom, what did you do that for?"

"My hand slipped."

"It did not. You did it on purpose. If your hand had slipped, you would have gone *honk*, one time, like that, instead of—"

"Well, she didn't look." They drove the rest of the way to the laundromat in silence. Bingo got out with the basket of laundry and entered.

There was one lady putting bedspreads in the oversized dryer, but she gave him only a disinterested glance. She did not have the look of a lady who had recently lost a load of sheets.

Bingo went down the line of washers, opening the lids and peering inside. In the fourth washer he recognized Jamie's sleepers, his father's worn underwear, diapers, his own T-shirt.

With a cry of relief, he took out the twisted laundry and replaced it with the stranger's twisted laundry.

With the basket on his hip, he rushed out the door and to the car.

"Go, Mom!" he cried as he slipped into the backseat and slammed the door.

She turned and looked at him. "You got the right laundry this time, Bingo?"

"Yes, Mom, yes! Go!"

"You're sure?"

"Yes! Look! Here's Dad's old underwear. Here are the diapers. Here's my SCUM T-shirt."

"And you put the other laundry back?"

"Yes, go! Go!"

And with what seemed to Bingo incredible slowness, his mother stepped on the gas.

The One-Way Disaster

"This reminds me of being in high school," Bingo's mother said as she tore through an intersection.

"Mom, watch what you're doing!"

"Frances Mimms and I used to trail Binkie Bambridge to see if he was two-timing her."

"Mom, watch it!"

Bingo was genuinely alarmed. Suddenly it had become his mother who was determined to find Melissa. She was almost in a frenzy. Bingo began to believe the shock she had had was more serious than his.

Bingo's brother had fallen asleep, but every time his mother took a corner too fast, he sucked on his pacifier as if he knew this careening was not ordinary behavior.

"Mom, can we go home, please?"

"I want to try one more street. They could have turned

down Madison." She applied the brakes. "I can't turn, though! It's one-way!"

"Mom, it is one-way *our* way," he explained with patience.

"No, Monroe's one-way our way. Madison's—"

"Mom, look at the sign. Look—at—the—sign. And if you're going to turn, you better get over in the other lane! Mom, now you've missed it."

"I deliberately missed it because I am going to turn onto Monroe, which is one-way *our* way!"

"Mom!"

"Trust me."

She made the turn, and they faced a solid line of oncoming cars. "Bingo, you were right," she cried. "It is one-way. And the stupid idiots are not going to let me through."

"Mom, we are the stupid idiots."

"Well, what should I do? Back up?"

People began blowing their horns, and his mom—never one to miss an opportunity—blew back.

Jamie awoke, sensed the general air of panic, spit out his pacifier, and began to wail—exactly what Bingo himself felt like doing.

"See what's wrong with the baby."

"The same thing is wrong with Jamie that's wrong with me—he doesn't like sitting here facing the wrong way on a one-way street. Mom, what's wrong with you? Let's go home."

"Well, there's no reason for it to be one-way." She leaned on the horn to show her displeasure.

"Mom, back into the K Mart parking lot if you can."

"Watch for me."

As she backed into the parking lot and stopped, she cried, "There they are, Bingo! We didn't miss them after all! They're in front of K Mart!"

Bingo poked Jamie's pacifier back in his mouth.

"This is the most excitement I've had since the baby came, which gives you some idea of how dull my life has become."

Bingo slumped down in the backseat.

"Maybe we should just sit here a minute until I calm down. Do you mind?"

"Not at all," Bingo said.

"I can't believe they made Monroe one-way. I never have been able to keep my presidents straight. So, where did they go?"

"Melissa and her friend? I don't know. Mom, are you calm enough to go home now?"

"You've seen enough?"

"Yes."

"You could run into K Mart. I could use extra diapers."

"No."

"Well, if you're sure . . ."

She started the car.

To fill in the time, Bingo began to work on his latest

problem. He wished he had paper so he could get it down while it was still fresh in his mind.

> *Problem #4. Unreliable Parent.*
> Suppose that you are in the car with a parent, and out the window you see a girl you love, and this girl will be in town for a short time and you don't know where she is staying and this is your one chance to find out. You are desperate. Is there any point in asking your parent to follow this girl to her place of residence?

> *Bingo's Answer:* No! Particularly not if the parent has suffered a recent shock of some undisclosed nature that will lead her to honk the horn inappropriately and go the wrong way on one-way streets. The best plan is to get out of the car as soon as she brings it to a safe stop and follow on foot. That is what I wish I had done.

When he had completed this thought Bingo looked up. He found to his surprise that they were still in the parking lot.

In the front seat his mother was slumped down in a dejected way.

"Mom, aren't we going home?"

"Eventually."

"What's wrong?"

She put her hands on the steering wheel. "Oh, I guess I'm stalling."

"Stalling? What for? What do you mean?"

"I don't want to go home."

"But why not? Mom, you might as well tell me what the shock was."

"Your father's novel came back today."

"His what?"

"His novel, Bingo, his novel! The novel he's been working on for years. *Bustin' Lewis*."

"I didn't even know he'd sent it to a publisher."

"He didn't want you to know. He was afraid you'd worry."

"But maybe I could have helped him."

"Maybe . . . He sent it in two weeks ago, Bingo, and he was so hopeful, and it's already come back. They didn't even have time to read it. I know they didn't."

"Maybe they liked it, Mom. They read it and liked it so much that they hurried to—"

She shook her head.

"They could have. I liked it."

"If they had liked it, they would have written or phoned. They wouldn't have sent it straight back."

Bingo took in this hurtful truth in silence.

"Somebody told me one time," his mother went on, "that the publishers have readers, and to save time the readers go through a manuscript and read every tenth page. Every tenth page! So maybe there would be nine perfect pages and then the tenth one would be—oh, I could just cry, Bingo."

"Please don't."

There was a long, shaky pause.

"Well, if I am going to cry, I wish I'd go ahead and do it and get it out of my system."

Bingo waited.

"Give me one more minute."

"Sure."

"I cry so seldom that it's hard for me to cry, even when I really need to. I have to really make an effort."

She kept her face forward.

"And I need to now."

Bingo felt it would have taken no effort at all for him to burst into tears, but somebody in the family had to be dry-eyed.

"My problem is that I just cannot bear to see your father hurt. He's such a wonderful man, Bingo, and I just—well, I'd rather be hurt myself."

The pacifier popped out of Jamie's mouth, and Bingo poked it back in.

Finally his mother did what Bingo had been praying she would do. She looked at her watch.

"So. Your father probably got home at five. He's now had thirty minutes to open the manuscript, read the letter, and absorb the disappointment. Do you think that's enough time?"

"I don't know. It probably wouldn't be for me."

"Well, we can't sit here forever."

"No, that's true."

She shoved the car into gear angrily. "Let's go home."

They drove home without speaking. As they turned onto the street his mother broke the silence.

"Now, Bingo, don't let on that I told you."

"I won't."

"Pretend you don't even know he sent it off."

"I will."

"His car's there. Oh, Bingo, I just can't bear it. He knows."

Rip Van Wentworth

Bingo was in his room. He had spent a lot of time in his room since he and his mother had gotten home yesterday.

He had come out for supper and breakfast, and every time the phone rang to see if Melissa was calling, but each time he went right back into his room. This was to give his father a chance to absorb his disappointment in privacy. Bingo understood the need for privacy, because he needed much more of it than he got.

So far his father had not finished absorbing, and each meal had been tedious. His mother kept saying things like, "Oh, Bingo, tell your dad who you saw in the store."

"Melissa."

"Who?" His father's face would be blank, as if his entire personality had left him.

"Melissa."

"Oh, Melissa. That's nice."

"Bingo! Tell your dad about the one-way street yesterday."

"Dad, we went down a one-way street yesterday."

"What?"

"A one-way street—the wrong way."

"That's nice."

While Bingo was sitting in his room, listening for a sound of normalcy from his father that would signal that the absorption period was over at last, Bingo suddenly remembered something Wentworth had said.

Something about Melissa . . .

Bingo had to think back hard to get it word for word because so much had happened in the meantime.

"And I know something else about Melissa," Wentworth had said, "but it'll cost you."

That was it exactly.

Bingo got up. Slowly he crossed to his window, bent, and looked out. He glanced across the lawn to Wentworth's bedroom window.

This was the low point in a week filled with low points. This might even be the low point of his life. Bingo opened the window, crawled out, crossed the lawn, and stopped at Wentworth's window.

He took a deep breath. He needed a lot of air because he was now in a place he had never thought he would be in his entire life. And he was doing the most alien thing he had ever done in his life.

But he had to do this. He had no other choice. He had to know what Wentworth knew about Melissa. It was more than a want, it was a burning desire, the kind he used to have so frequently.

He lifted his hand and knocked.

Wentworth's face appeared in the window almost immediately.

"Who is it?"

Wentworth peered through the glass. Bingo knew Wentworth could see him, but Wentworth, out of cruelty, feigned temporary blindness.

"Me."

"Me who?"

"Me Bingo."

He cringed. He was starting to sound like a character in a Tarzan movie. "Bingo Brown," he added with dignity.

"What are you doing out there?"

"I wanted to talk to you."

"You want to talk to somebody, you come to the front door, you call them up on the phone. You don't wake them up in the middle of the afternoon."

"Wentworth, you've been knocking on my window for over a year now, and I have been very, very patient with you."

"That's what's wrong with you, Worm Brain, you're too patient. Somebody knocks at my window—I don't want to talk to them, I shut the window."

Wentworth closed the window, and Bingo stood without moving. A sudden breeze brought goosebumps to his bare arms. All month the weather had been seesawing between summer and winter, and now it had made up its mind. Leaves began raining from the trees.

Bingo turned and started back to his house. Through the rustle of falling leaves, he heard the window open behind him.

He didn't turn around but he found himself taking smaller steps.

"So, I'm curious," Wentworth said to Bingo's back.

"Oh?" Bingo stopped in place and put his hands in his pockets. Bingo was very grateful for pockets. He never had anything of value to put in them, but his hands had spent their only really restful moments there. Like now, if his hands hadn't been in his pockets, they would have been twitching nervously at his sides.

Wentworth continued. "What'd you want to see me about?"

"About something you said—"

Bingo still did not turn around.

"I say a lot of things."

"This was yesterday afternoon when you came back out of the grocery store. You told me you'd seen Melissa."

"I had seen her."

"I know. And later you came over and knocked on *my* window"—Bingo threw this in as a reminder—"and

I answered and you said you knew something about Melissa but it would cost me?"

"Yeah?"

"What's the price?"

"The price is that you'll owe me—like in the Mafia. You'll owe me and you'll owe me and then one day I'll come up and say, 'I'm collecting,' and you'll have to do whatever I say."

"Forget it."

"It wouldn't be murder, Bingo, I wouldn't ask you to rub somebody out."

"Forget it!"

"Even though my history teacher is asking for it. He calls me Rip Van Wentworth because—he claims—I slept through his entire reading of the Declaration of Independence."

"Forget it!"

Bingo started for home.

"Okay, okay, I must be getting soft, but I'll tell you what you want to know."

Bingo stopped. This time he turned. He waited, still suspicious. This could be another of Wentworth's cruelties.

"I know where Melissa's at. I know approximately where she's at. I can take you there."

"Where?"

"She's at her cousin's."

"I didn't know she had a cousin."

"That was who was with her in the store—her cousin. Name's Zelda Louise, but she gets mad if you don't call her Weezie."

"So is she here for a visit or what?"

"Nobody said, but I get the feeling she's moving back."

"Melissa's moving back?"

"Well, maybe. Like I said, 'Melissa, you moving back?' And Zelda Louise gives me a look like that is not a good question to be asking. Her dad probably lost his job again."

"I thought her dad had a good job in Bixby."

"He did."

"So what makes you think he lost it?"

"Nothing, Worm Brain, nothing. I'm giving you an opinion, like on the evening news."

"He lost his job . . ." Bingo trailed off thoughtfully. His heart clutched the news.

No wonder Melissa hadn't called him, hadn't written. She would naturally have wanted to spare him the hurt and—

But surely she knew by now that he would like nothing better than to help her over any hurt that life dealt her.

"You want to go over there?" Wentworth continued, getting ready to pull his camouflage T-shirt on over his head. He peered at Bingo through the neck opening.

"Where?"

"To the cousin's, Worm Brain! To Zelda Louise's."

"Now?"

"No, Worm Brain, next Fourth of July." Wentworth pulled on his shirt and ran his hands over his military haircut. "Yeah, now," he said, shaking his head at Bingo's stupidity. "Get your bike and I'll meet you out front."

Merrily We Burp Along

"Burp-burp *burp* burp . . . burp-burp *burp* burp." Billy Wentworth stopped his series of burps to ask, "So, what song is that the beginning of?"

"I don't know," Bingo admitted. In moments of frivolity he enjoyed body noises as much as anybody, but he was not feeling frivolous now.

"You gotta know. It's a golden oldie. Wait, I'll do it again."

"Please don't," Bingo said. "I haven't had any lunch and—"

"Burp-burp *burp* burp . . . Some of my burps come up better than others, but you get the picture."

Bingo and Wentworth were pedaling slowly toward Weezie's house. To pass the time, Wentworth was burp-singing popular hits.

". . . burp-burp *burp* burp. I'll give you one more hint. It's by the Rolling Stones. I'll do it again, and this is your last chance."

"I won't know it no matter how many times you do it."

"You better know it. Like, it's a game, Worm Brain. You gotta get the song or I don't tell you whether to go right or left at the next corner."

"Wentworth, I can't concentrate."

The reason that Bingo was unable to concentrate was that he was composing a problem, and it was a problem he was soon to face.

Problem #5. Seeing Long-Lost Girlfriend.
Suppose you are in love with a girl and suppose you have not seen this girl in a long time because events beyond your control have kept you apart. The last time you saw this girl, you did not attempt to embrace her because the two of you were in Health Supplies, and your arms wouldn't work right. This time your arms probably won't work right either and although there won't be any health supplies to deter you, there will be someone present who would like it if your arms didn't work right. Should you—

Bingo broke off. This was not like a problem, this was more like the rambling of an addled mind. And Bingo did not want to encourage such ramblings in his baby brother. Manfully, he broke off his thoughts.

"Well, if you can't concentrate," Wentworth said, "I'll give you a hint. Burp-burp *burp* burp sat-is-*fac*-tion. Get it?"

"I got it."

"Turn left."

They made the corner.

"Weezie lives on this street—I don't know the exact number. Melissa said, 'I'm staying with my cousin until my dad . . . er, works things out.' And Weezie—who, incidentally, had not taken her eyes off me—that girl's got taste—says, 'I live on Duquesne.' Like she would not be unhappy if I made my way to Duquesne—" He broke off.

"This has got to be it," Bingo said.

"Why?"

"Because there's Weezie."

"Where?"

"On the steps."

"That's not Weezie. Weezie doesn't go around with doohickeys on her head."

"She's getting a home perm. That's what they bought in the grocery store. When she gets through her hair will be curly, like Melissa's."

"Man, I'm sorry I saw that."

"Well, you wait here. I'll go the rest of the way by myself."

"No, I can take it. She must want to see me bad to come outside with those doohickeys on her head."

Bingo and Wentworth walked their bikes up the sidewalk to where Weezie sat on the steps. She was flipping through a magazine and didn't look up.

"Hi," Bingo said.

Now she noticed them. "Oh, hi."

Bingo filled in the silence with a loud swallow and then blurted out, "I saw you and Melissa in the grocery store."

The cousin came back with, "I saw you see us."

Bingo did not care for mixed-sex conversations that started like this, but he had no choice but to continue.

"That *was* Melissa, then?"

"It was Melissa."

"So where is she now?"

"Inside."

"Is she coming out?"

"No."

"Why not?"

"There's no reason for her to come out."

There was another silence. Bingo sensed that Weezie had intended this as an insult, but he forced himself to say, "Would you ask her to come out?"

"No."

"Why not?"

"Look, Weez," Wentworth said, interrupting impatiently. "I don't want to break up this exciting conversation here, but Bingo came over to see Melissa. And I came over to make sure he sees Melissa. And if you don't get Melissa out here, it's going to be a long afternoon, because we ain't leaving until he sees Melissa, and Bingo and me got better things to do."

Bingo was grateful to Billy Wentworth. Sometimes a forceful manner was necessary, and Bingo obviously wasn't up to force of any kind.

"Me-liiissa!" she called.

"That's more like it," Wentworth said. He tugged down his camouflage T-shirt in a satisfied manner.

"What do you want?" Melissa called back.

Her voice was so close at hand that Bingo thought she must have been standing by the window all along. He glanced quickly at the window and thought he saw the curtain move. He wished he hadn't come.

"Somebody wants to see-eee you!" Weezie called over her shoulder.

"Who?"

"Bingo Bro-own."

"Tell him I'll be out in a minute."

"She'll be out in a minute."

"We ain't deaf," Wentworth said.

"Let's go," Bingo said.

Wentworth ignored him. "I want to get something straight here, Zelda Louise."

"How do you know my name?"

"I got my sources."

"Who?"

"I never reveal a source."

"I hate to be called Zelda Louise. Now, you call me Weezie or I'm going in the house and I'm never coming out."

Wentworth waved an imaginary white flag. "Weezie," he said. "Weezie, here's what I want to get straight. Are we talking a regular minute, sixty seconds, or one of those minutes that takes about an hour and a half? Because me and Bingo do not have an hour and a half to waste."

"Let's go!" Bingo said.

Bingo didn't think he could stand this any longer. The confusion, the anxiety, were beginning to take their toll. He needed to sink down on his Ninja Turtle sheets and stay there, Rip Van Bingo–like, for at least forty years.

Also he hadn't had any lunch, and his stomach was getting ready to start growling.

"No, hold on," Wentworth said. "She said one minute. So, we'll give her one minute. I figure fifteen seconds of the minute is gone already, so we now wait forty-five seconds."

Wentworth checked his watch. "Forty-one . . . thirty-eight . . . thirty . . . twenty-two . . . nineteen . . . thirteen . . . eight . . . three . . . two . . . one and a half . . ."

Bingo waited without hope.

And when Billy Wentworth said, "One and one-quarter," Bingo heard the front door open.

He looked up so fast his neck popped.

There, in the doorway, wearing her Declaration of Independence T-shirt, stood Melissa.

Melissa, at Last

"So, Weez!" Billy Wentworth said.

Now that Melissa had put in an appearance, Wentworth turned his full attention to Weezie.

"When are you going to get them doohickeys off your head?"

Weezie checked her bare wrist and circled it with her other hand. "I keep forgetting my watch is broken," she said. "I have to wait about ten more minutes. It's already been neutralized."

"Man, if I had them doohickeys on my head, I wouldn't wait to be nooo-tralized. I bet them things hurt, don't they?"

"A little bit," she admitted.

"I figured."

"These on my neck are rolled real tight."

Neither Bingo nor Melissa had spoken—Bingo because he couldn't, Melissa because she wouldn't. She was still standing just outside the front door, turned sideways.

Bingo had been looking at her ever since she came outside, but she had continued to look down at her shoes.

Bingo glanced at her shoes himself to see what was so fascinating. They weren't her old shoes. They were new and, as he had expected, larger in size.

Then he looked up so quickly he caught her looking at him. But at once she looked away, and he did, too. He had an uneasy, guilty feeling, as if he were back in Puritan times, when even a look was illegal.

"Wait till you see me tomorrow," Weezie said to Wentworth in a flirtatious manner. "You'll think it was worth it."

"Nothing's worth putting them doohickeys on your head for. I wouldn't put them things on my head if it would make me look like Arnold Schwarzenegger."

Weezie laughed through her nose. Bingo's mother had been right. She did snort.

Bingo slowly raised his eyes to Melissa's face. She, too, had just raised her eyes to Bingo's face, but again she looked away. This time Bingo fixed his eyes on her face in a manly manner. He would not look away, no matter what.

"Boys do get home perms these days," Weezie told Wentworth.

"Well, that's so fascinating I'll write that down in my diary tonight."

"They do!"

"Not me!"

"You could."

"No way!"

"Why not? You'd be cute with curly hair."

"I ain't denying that."

"You buy the home perm and I'll give you one. I've got the curlers."

"No way."

"Please."

"No! Now, I'm not getting no home permanent, no matter how much you beg."

Bingo couldn't believe what was happening. Here he was—the master of mixed-sex conversations—unable to speak a word. And here was Wentworth sounding like he had invented mixed-sex conversations.

A small silence followed, and Bingo heard Melissa exhale.

When Bingo heard that, he knew that she had been holding her breath. He had been doing the exact same thing.

This gave him courage. Now was the time to speak. He moistened his dry lips.

His stomach rumbled like a volcano.

It could not possibly have happened at a worse moment. This stomach growl could only make Melissa think he was hungry. Then she would remember his love letter for eternity in which he had written so eloquently of the hunger of love. And she would not linger over the poignant closing—"Hungrily yours." She would go directly on to remember that she had received the Xerox of that letter.

Then she would go in the house.

So he had to speak. Otherwise, he had made this long, torturous, burp-ridden trip for nothing. He would say something simple and truthful.

"I was surprised to see you in Health Supplies yesterday."

"Oh, hi, Bingo."

Encouraged, Bingo went up two steps. "Hi. I was getting ready to write you a letter."

"Were you?"

"Yes. Only then I saw you and I knew I didn't need to write. I could just tell you."

"Tell me what?"

Bingo felt as if he were talking to a stranger. "Things."

"Like what?"

"Well, for one thing, remember the last letter I wrote?"

"I don't remember. It's been so long. I haven't gotten a letter in three months."

"Me either."

"Oh, I do remember. It was Xeroxed."

"Yes, but—"

"Because it was the first Xeroxed letter I ever got."

"I can explain that."

"And you don't forget Xeroxed letters."

"Apparently not."

"They're like—so impersonal—like, I don't know—form letters."

"Zelda Lou-iiiise!" a voice called from inside the house.

Weezie made a face. "What, Claudine Shirley?" she called back.

"You wanted me to let you know when it was eleven-thirty, Zelda Louise. Well, it's eleven-thirty."

"Thanks." Weezie got to her feet. "I've got to go in and"—she laughed out of her nose—"get these doohickeys out of my hair."

"It's about time."

"Come on, Melissa, help me," Weezie said.

Weezie crossed to the front door. Melissa was standing there, looking once again at her shoes.

Weezie looked over her shoulder. "Come back tomorrow," she told Wentworth, "and see my curls."

"Maybe I will. Maybe I won't," Wentworth said. "I don't make no promises."

"I bet you come."

Weezie went into the house with a sassy wave of her hand to Wentworth. Melissa followed without any signal at all.

Bingo stood without moving. They—the all-time champions of mixed-sex conversations—had lost their title. The words "form letter" had hurt him. He was as tired as if he'd been pumping iron.

Wentworth got on his bicycle and Bingo, robotlike, did, too.

"So what's wrong?" Wentworth asked. "You wanted to see Melissa, you got to see her."

"Right."

"So what's wrong?"

"I didn't find out anything, Wentworth. I don't know any more than I did. I don't know if Melissa's here for a visit or here to stay or what."

"You should have asked," Wentworth said. "You want to know something, Worm Brain, you ask. Remember that from now on."

"I'll try."

"How'd you ever get in the gifted program in school?"

"I honestly don't know."

"What do you do in there, anyway?"

"Read."

"That's it?"

"Pretty much. Read and talk about what we read."

"I tell you one thing—I sure am glad I ain't gifted." Wentworth leaned back on his bicycle seat. "Here's my rule about grades. You could learn from this. The only grade I want is C+. B is wimpy. D gets me grief at home. If you get an A, you've been wasting your time. And if I get a C, and it ain't got a plus after it, I put one."

They continued to pedal toward home.

Wentworth said, "You want to go back over to Weezie's tomorrow?"

Bingo said, "No."

"I don't either, but I figure you got to."

"Why?"

"Look, you bombed out. That was obvious. And when you bomb out, Worm Brain, you have to try again real quick or you'll end up bonkers."

Bingo pedaled faster.

"Don't worry," Wentworth said, pulling up beside him, "I'll see that you come and I'll give you my personal guarantee not to let you look stupid no matter how stupid you look."

Bingo said, "Thanks a lot."

"This'll cheer you up. Burp burp burp-burp-burp. You gotta get this song." He glanced at Bingo and said, "It's your song, Worm Brain. Burp burp burp-burp-burp, and Bingo was his name-o!"

Bingo Brown and the Brownettes

Problem #6. Saturday Inertia.

Suppose you wake up one Saturday morning and you do not feel exhilarated, as you usually do on Saturday mornings. Indeed, you don't even want to watch cartoons. Can this be due to love?

Bingo's Answer: Definitely. This is known as unrequited love, and it is one of the least fortunate types of love. It is better to have no love than unrequited—

"Oh, Bingo, come here a minute."

Bingo put down his pencil.

"Hurry, Bingo, I've got something I want to show you."

Dutifully, Bingo got up and went down the hall. He stood in the doorway to his mother's room, leaning against the sill.

"What?"

His mother was sitting on the edge of the bed. Beyond her lay his father with his eyes closed, his freckled hands folded at his waist. He was still trying to absorb his disappointment.

"I just wrote something in Jamie's baby book," his mother said with what sounded like false cheer. "Want to hear it?"

"I guess."

"This is under 'Firsts'—you know, like first step, first tooth—which, incidentally, I'm still waiting for, Gummy."

This was directed to Jamie. She lifted him in the air, and he drooled with delight.

"You need teeth, because teeth dam up the drool, yes, they do!"

Bingo continued to wait in the doorway until she turned back to him.

"Anyway, this *is* a first—of sorts. Here's what I wrote, Bingo. 'First time going wrong way on a one-way street. Occasion: Chasing brother's girlfriend . . .' "

"Oh, Mom."

"Wait, Bingo, there's more. It gets funnier."

But Bingo had had all the humor he could stand. He started for his room.

"Oh, by the by," his mother called after him. "Did you see Melissa?"

"Yes."

"What did she have to say?"

"Not much."

"When you grow up, Gummy," she said, dismissing Bingo, "I hope you're going to have a better sense of humor than your big brother!"

Bingo went into his room and lay down on his bed. He closed his eyes.

He was asleep in seconds, and he was in luck. His favorite dream began at once.

In the dream Bingo was on a stage. It was obviously him onstage, and yet it was a more mature, handsome version of himself. It was Bingo Brown at, oh, age twenty, and Bingo was very pleased at the way his form and features had shaped up.

He needed a dream like this.

He was a famous singer, and his backup group was the Brownettes. Bingo Brown and the Brownettes. The dream was so pleasant and full of promise that Bingo came partially awake, but he forced himself to go back to sleep.

The audience was calling for him. "Bin-go! Bin-go! Bin-go! Bin-go!"

It made him love his name and everything else about himself.

Then, without warning, the dream fast-forwarded and

became a nightmare. He was onstage, but the Brownettes had turned against him.

> Me-lissa's back and Bingo doesn't have her.
> Nyah nyah, nyah nyah, nyah-nyah-nyah, nyah.

Bingo groaned in his sleep. A hand gripped his shoulder. Now his mother was in the dream, saying, "Can I ask a big favor?"

"Get off the stage, Mom, before the audience sees you. It's—"

"Bingo!"

"What? What?"

He struggled back to consciousness.

"Bingo, your dad and I want to get out of the house. Will you watch Jamie, please?"

"How long have I been asleep?"

"I don't know—two or three minutes. Will you watch Jamie?"

"Mom, I've got to read *The Red Badge of Courage* for English. I haven't even gotten to the war yet."

She made a worried face and turned her eyes back toward the bedroom where his father still lay. "Your dad is really depressed," she whispered. "I've got to get him out of the house. So will you watch Jamie?"

She lowered her voice again. Bingo could barely hear her himself now.

"Please, Bingo, I'm worried about your father." She

sank down on the edge of Bingo's bed. "You know what the rejection letter said?"

Bingo shook his head. "No."

"It was just one sentence, Bingo. One sentence! 'We have read your manuscript and regret that it does not meet the needs of our list.' What does that mean, Bingo—'meet the needs of our list'?"

"I don't know."

"All those hours and hours of work and it doesn't meet the needs of their list."

Her shoulders sagged.

Bingo cleared his throat. She looked at him with quick hope, so Bingo said, "Maybe he should send it off again. There are other—lists."

"I couldn't suggest it."

"Mom, if you bomb out, you have to try again quickly or you'll go bonkers." Now Bingo was quoting Wentworth.

"Bingo, he just lies there like he's in his coffin, with his hands folded like this."

She folded her hands pitifully at her waist.

Bingo sighed. "How long will you be gone?" he said because it seemed to him his mother was sinking into depression, too. Then the whole family would be depressed—except for Jamie.

"Two hours. Is that too long? Can you watch him for two hours?"

"I guess."

"Now I've got to convince your dad to go out—and that's not going to be easy. Where can we go? Bingo, I can't even think of anywhere we can go!"

"I can't help you there."

"It's got to be somewhere vital. I can't just say the store or the movies or the laundromat. Well, I'll think of something."

El Bingo, the Gringo

Bingo was walking slowly down the hall toward English class when he heard someone call his name.

"Bingo, wait up!"

Bingo glanced over his shoulder.

"Wait!"

It was Mamie Lou, and Bingo did not like to talk to Mamie Lou even when he was feeling his best—which he definitely was not.

He tried to slip into class, but in one quick move she was in front of him, blocking the way. Since Mamie Lou had him by twenty pounds, he had no choice but to stop.

"Yes, Mamie Lou?"

"Did you see Melissa?" she asked excitedly.

"Yes, I saw her Saturday—and briefly Sunday, but I didn't get to really talk to her."

"No, I mean now," Mamie Lou said. She pointed down the hall as if she were thumbing a ride. "Did you just see her in the hall?"

"No, no, I didn't. She's here? At school?"

"Yes, but there were about two hundred people around her. You'd think she'd been to the moon instead of Bixby, Oklahoma. I barely got to say hi."

"I didn't get much past that myself." Bingo turned. "Where exactly was she? Maybe if I—"

"Mamie Lou, you and—who's that behind you?" Mr. Rodrigo called from his desk.

Bingo peered around her.

"Ah, El Bingo, the Gringo," Mr. Rodrigo said. "You two come on in, we'd like to get started."

"Mr. Rodrigo." Bingo paused in the doorway. "I have a compelling errand. I wouldn't use the word *compelling*, which means to drive or urge irresistibly, if I weren't being driven and urged irresistibly."

"*No comprendo,* Bingo."

When Mr. Rodrigo switched to what he called his "native tongue," even the correct use of a word wouldn't divert him.

Bingo proceeded reluctantly into the room. He sat at his desk. He wanted to put his head on his desk, because the wood would be cooler than his flushed face, but Mr. Rodrigo didn't allow siestas.

Bingo was ashamed of himself. Only yesterday he had sworn that he would never, ever care about Melissa again, that he would not so much as go to the door if she rang the doorbell, and here he was with his heart leaping out of his chest because she was in the same building with him.

This decision that he would never care again had come yesterday. He and Wentworth had returned to Weezie's only to find the house locked.

"Maybe Weezie and Melissa are hiding inside," Bingo had said.

"Maybe Melissa's hiding from you. She did that yesterday. But there's no way the Weez would hide from me."

Wentworth had continued to punch the doorbell for some time, even after Bingo had begged him to stop. Finally Wentworth had said, "Okay, okay, I give up."

They had turned and started down the steps. At that moment a car had pulled into the driveway. Bingo and Wentworth stopped to watch.

The backseat of the car had been so filled with girls of assorted ages and sizes that Bingo couldn't be sure Melissa was one of them. She was. She was the third girl out of the car. Weezie was the fourth. The rest of the girls kept coming, like clowns piling out of a circus car.

Weezie had seen them and at once threw up her hands for protection. "Don't look at my hair. It looks awful. Melissa, don't let them look at my hair. Don't look!"

Melissa had gotten between Weezie and the boys on the steps, and they ran into the house.

It had been so sudden that Bingo and Wentworth continued to stand there, stunned, while the rest of the girls passed by.

Finally, Bingo had called, "Melissa!"

And Wentworth had helped with, "Come on out, Melissa, or Bingo's going to leave."

Silence.

"And he's not coming back either."

Silence.

"And bring the Weez with you, or I'm leaving with him."

In a lower voice, Wentworth had said, "Do you think they're coming out?"

"I don't know, what do you think?"

"I don't know."

"You've got a sister," Bingo said finally. "Would she come out?"

"My sister would never have gone in. Her hair looks like that all the time."

Still they had waited. And as Bingo stood there, trapped by desire and confusion, he had made a firm, mature decision. He would never attempt to see Melissa again—ever!

"I'm leaving," Bingo had said then.

"I'm right behind you."

And now, twenty-four hours later, he was ready to skip class and rush through the empty halls in the hope of catching a glimpse of her.

The class had begun to discuss *The Red Badge of Courage*. Bingo got out his book.

Mamie Lou was saying, "You know what I don't understand, Mr. Rodrigo? You know how everyone is always telling us to write about what we know? Well, Stephen Crane wasn't writing about what he knew. He never even went to war!"

Usually Bingo liked to jump in with an opinion, but he had only read chapter one, and it had taken him all evening to read that.

The trouble was that Bingo had kept coming to sentences so full of meaning that they would send him off on a personal detour. He would read, "The youth was in a little trance of astonishment." And he would be taken back to Health Supplies, where he, himself, had suffered a little trance of astonishment. And he would relive the little trance in detail.

He would force himself to read on, but he would come to something like, "He departed feeling vague relief," and he would be leaving Weezie's yesterday with his own vague relief.

He would read about the youth feeling gratitude for the words of his comrade, and he would again hear Wentworth saying, "I'm right behind you."

He would read of the youth staring steadfastly at the dark girl while she stared up through the high tree branches at the sky, and he would be staring steadfastly at Melissa, who was staring steadfastly at her shoes.

"Well, El Bingo, the Gringo, is strangely silent today," Mr. Rodrigo said.

Bingo glanced up from his book. "I haven't gotten as far in the book as the rest of the class," he explained.

"You're my fastest reader, Bingo. You're always leading the pack."

"I know."

"So what? It didn't grab you?"

"It wasn't that. I kept . . . stopping to think."

An amused murmur came from some of the gifted and talented who rarely did that themselves.

Mr. Rodrigo ignored them. "So you were *simpático* with the main character?"

Bingo thought about it. "I guess. I kept coming to these sentences that seemed to fit . . . me."

"So, class—no, put your hand down, Mamie Lou, it's my turn. So while Stephen Crane had not been to war, he did know—and quite well—what it was like to be a young man facing a turning point in his life. He knew what it was like to have a mother who loved him but didn't understand him enough to say what he really needed to hear her say.

"He knew what it was to yearn for a girl he couldn't

have. He knew what it was to worry about his abilities. That's what Bingo, in his own inimitable fashion, was trying to tell us. Eh, Gringo?"

Bingo was grateful to Mr. Rodrigo for turning him from the class idiot into the class intelligensio. A kind teacher could work miracles.

"*Si*," he said.

The Red Badge
of Spaghetti

The Brown family was having spaghetti for supper, and supper had been served. But the only sounds in the kitchen were the slaps of Jamie's hands against his high-chair tray.

Jamie did not know spaghetti was to be eaten. He thought you slapped at it in a violent way and, later, when tired of the violence, swept it off the tray onto the floor.

"Many writers," Bingo said finally, "go unappreciated in their lifetimes."

Bingo was not displeased with this opening statement. He felt it was rare that anyone under stress, as he himself was, could break a painful silence with a remark of intelligence and depth.

"What's that supposed to mean?" Bingo's father asked, looking up sharply. His long days in the house had given him a pallor that made his freckles seem darker than usual.

"Nothing. Nothing!" Bingo said, at once aware his remark had gone unappreciated.

He had spoken only as a favor—to break the terrible silence that hovered over the table. He still wasn't supposed to know that his father's manuscript had been rejected, but his father took any literary comment as a personal insult.

Bingo's mother gave him a warning look.

Bingo cleared his throat. "We're reading *The Red Badge of Courage,* that's all, and Stephen Crane died real young."

The conversation also died young, and once again the only sounds were Jamie slapping his spaghetti. Bingo had with great patience taught Jamie to say bye-bye, but like a parrot, Jamie said it inappropriately. Now, as he karate-chopped the spaghetti, which refused to be chopped, he cried, "Bye-bye-bye-bye."

"But I despair of finishing the book," Bingo continued.

No one asked the reason for this despair.

Bingo had begun chapter two when he got home from school and had almost immediately come across the paragraph, "For days he made ceaseless calculations, but they were all wondrously unsatisfactory. He found that he could establish nothing."

As soon as he had read that he realized that he, himself, had also established exactly nothing.

Problem #7. Establishing Exactly Nothing.
Suppose you have seen a person you love and no matter how hard you try, you have found no answers and established nothing. Should you then continue to pursue this person until your questions are answered?

Bingo's Answer: Yes! Or until she is no longer in the area.

"Stephen Crane died young, but not unappreciated," his father said.

Bingo said, "Oh?"

"At least he got published."

"Ah," Bingo said.

The rest of the meal was eaten in silence, except for the sounds of Jamie attacking spaghetti.

Sometimes when Bingo watched his brother he wished he were little again and could find simple pleasure in slapping spaghetti or comfort in holding the end of a frayed blanket. Once he had even put Jamie's pacifier in his mouth, but he had taken it out as soon as he saw his reflection in the mirror.

In these moments, he tried to remind himself of the long and difficult road from where Jamie sat in his high chair to where he himself sat in a straight chair.

At last Bingo's father got up from the table. "That was good."

"You hardly ate anything, Sam."

"I'm just not that hungry."

"You have to eat."

"I'll put my plate in the fridge and heat it up later."

When his father was gone, Bingo's mother hissed, "Why did you do that?" It was a hard sentence to hiss because it didn't have any *s*'s in it, but she managed.

"Do what? What did I do?"

"Bring up writing."

"I was lucky to think of it. Maybe you two can sit in silence for the rest of your lives, but I need sounds."

"Your father was just beginning to come out of his depression. Now I have to start cheering him up all over again. Clean the kitchen."

"Mom, I have got to read my book."

"Do that after you clean the kitchen."

"Bye-bye," Jamie said.

"I wish," Bingo answered.

He got up slowly. He glanced down at his shirt, at the red spaghetti sauce over his heart, and he began to clear the table.

When he finished the kitchen he took Jamie, wiped his hands, and went back to his book. He did something he rarely did—turned to the end.

There he read a wonderful sentence. "Listen to this," he told his brother. " 'He felt a quiet manhood, not assertive but of sturdy and strong blood.' "

He looked at the back of his brother's neck, a sight

that always made him feel protective of his brother. "That's what I want to feel."

Jamie yawned. Bingo felt a flow of affection as pure and uncomplicated as affection is supposed to be.

"And here's something else. 'Scars faded as flowers.' Ah. 'Scars faded as flowers.' Just between you and me, I have some scars that I wouldn't mind seeing fade as flowers."

Jamie lay back against him. He put one hand on his head and began to rub his hair.

"Oh, and listen to this. 'He turned with a lover's thirst to images of tranquil skies, fresh meadows, cool brooks—an existence of soft and eternal peace.' "

Bingo was prepared to take that sentence phrase by phrase, starting with a lover's thirst, about which he was something of an expert, but Jamie had already gone to sleep.

Quietly, Bingo took him to his room and laid him on his stomach in his crib.

"If I come to any other good parts that I think you'll enjoy, I'll read them to you tomorrow," he said.

The Unfortunate Facts

Bingo was used to facing unfortunate facts about himself. Only last week, before Melissa came, he had willingly, even good-naturedly, accepted that:

1. He was penniless.
2. He had only half a sentence on his essay for civics. "The study of civics is important because . . ."
3. He continued to gag every time he had to change a diaper.
4. Dark hair was growing on his toes. (And while he had used his dad's razor without permission a time or two, he was aware his dad would not want him to use it on his toes. He would not want to use his own razor, if he had one, on his toes.)

Now he was forced to add two new, even more unfortunate facts to the list, and he was not accepting them
good-naturedly or willingly.

    5. He was womanless.
    6. He had a depressed father.

Bingo was aware he couldn't do much about number
five. He felt Melissa was lost to him forever.

Yet he still longed for her and thought of her. She was
the only perfect girl he had ever known.

> *Problem #8. Following a Perfect Love.*
> Suppose that you have fallen in love with a girl
> who is perfect, and because of this, the love you
> shared was perfect. That love is now ended. Would
> it be cruel to allow another girl to fall in love with
> you, when you know it can be only an imperfect
> love?
>
> *Bingo's Answer:* I am not qualified at present to
> answer this, having not experienced imperfect love
> personally, but I will get back to this, for, like
> everything else, it will probably befall me.

Bingo couldn't do much to hurry the imperfect love
along, but there was something he could do about his
father.

His mother had left for the afternoon. She had to be

at the opening of some new town houses. But she had left specific instructions. "Listen for Jamie, and don't do anything to upset your father."

As soon as her car was out of sight, however, Bingo went to his parents' room. His father lay on the bed in his usual position, with his freckled hands folded on his chest.

"Dad, are you asleep?" Bingo asked from the doorway.

"Not quite."

"You want some company?"

"Oh, I don't know. Like who?"

"Me. Can I come in?"

"Sure."

Bingo came in and stood awkwardly beside the bed. He recalled that often his father had come into Bingo's room and stood this way as Bingo lay on his Smurf sheets. His father usually said, "Is there something troubling you, son? Is everything all right?"

But that wasn't Bingo's way. Bingo blurted out, "I know your manuscript got rejected."

There was a silence. Only the refolding of his father's long, freckled fingers showed that he had heard the statement.

Finally his father said, "I was going to get around to telling you."

"I just wanted to let you know that I know how it feels."

"Oh?"

"I sent one of my manuscripts off."

"I didn't know you'd ever finished one."

"Well, it wasn't finished. It was only one paragraph. It was the one that started out, 'At eight-thirty the earth beneath the city began to move. The tremor measured nine on the Richter scale. People thought it was an earthquake. The animals knew better. The animals knew that what had moved beneath the city was alive, alive after four thousand years of sleep! It was alive and it was coming up!' "

"You sent that off?"

"Yes, and I asked if they wanted to see the rest of the manuscript—I didn't mention the fact that I hadn't finished writing it, of course."

"What did they say?"

"Nothing. They just sent a printed slip of paper thanking me for sending it but saying they couldn't publish it. Later I discovered I had misspelled *Richter,* and of course that might have had something to do with their reluctance to publish."

"Perhaps. Have you sent off other things, Bingo?"

"No, that's the only one. I felt like my science-fiction story that takes place in Mau Mau really wasn't long enough."

"I've forgotten that one. Refresh my memory."

" 'Something was stirring deep within the volcano on the island of Mau Mau, and it was not lava.' "

His father seemed to control a smile. "It *is* sort of short."

"But I make every word count."

"I'll grant you that."

"If I can get a couple more paragraphs, I'll probably go ahead and put it in the mail. You need to send yours off again, Dad," Bingo said.

"I guess."

"You have to! I would send mine off a hundred times if I believed in it."

"You would, wouldn't you?"

"Yes."

"It's probably not so much that I wanted this manuscript to be published—although I did want that. I wanted a new way of life, Bingo. I wanted to stay home and write, but I can't do that if I can't justify it. If I can't sell something—if I can't make a living—then I can't sit around all day at the word processor."

"Send it off again."

"Well, I will. I need to read it over—maybe I can make it better."

"You want me to read it?"

"Oh, no, no, I think I've got to make my own decisions on this. I know you wouldn't want me fiddling with your Richter-scale monster. By the way, what is that thing that's coming up after four thousand years of sleep?"

"I don't know. When I figure it out, I'll let you know."

"You got anything else in the works?" his father asked.

"Well, I have two other science-fiction stories started, but lately I've been working on—"

He broke off as he thought of his *Guide to Romance*. He was, he thought, like a child who had briefly waded in the ocean attempting a book about swimming the Pacific.

"I've been working on something sort of personal."

"Anything you'd care to talk about?"

"Not really. But Dad, you know how they're always saying write about what you know?"

"Yes."

"Well, I was writing about what I thought I knew, only I didn't know as much as I thought I did. Some of my answers seem, well, less than perfect."

"That's hard to believe."

"It happens. Are you working on anything else, Dad?"

His father smiled. "Not anything I'd care to comment on."

"But you do have another idea?"

His smile remained. "I might as well admit it. I do have another idea."

The literary discussion was interrupted by a wail from down the hall.

"Well, I better go. That's Jamie. I told Mom I'd listen out for him."

Bingo's dad threw his long legs off the side of his bed.

"I'll get him. I've been sort of ignoring Jamie lately. You go on out and take the afternoon off."

Bingo Brown's Day Off

Bingo lay on the grass, listening to Billy Wentworth read *The Red Badge of Courage* aloud.

Bingo's eyes were closed.

Wentworth was not a good reader. " 'Hear th' news, boys? Corkright's crushed th' hull rebel right an' captured two hull divisions.' "

Wentworth stopped. "I wonder what a hull division is."

"How is it spelled?" Bingo asked without opening his eyes.

"*H-u-l-l.*"

"I think he means *whole*—whole division," Bingo explained.

"*Hull* is whole?"

"The character has an accent."

"I get it, but I don't like it. You get a lot of accents in Gifted and Talented?" he asked curiously.

"Enough."

"Then I'm glad I ain't gifted and talented. Where was I? Oh, here. 'I tell yeh'—*yeh* is *you*, right? I'm catching on to this. 'I tell yeh I've been all over that there ken-try.' Ken-try." He kept trying the word. "Ken-try."

"Country," Bingo said.

Bingo didn't understand how he had come to be lying on the grass, allowing Billy Wentworth to read aloud to him.

He had come into the backyard with *The Red Badge of Courage* under his arm. He had thought that a change of scene might help him concentrate. Certainly he was unable to concentrate on his Ninja Turtle sheets.

There was a tree in the backyard where Bingo, in his carefree younger days, had sat and read. He remembered pleasantly the rustling of the leaves around him, the comfort of the sturdy old tree limbs that seemed to envelop him, Disney-movie-like, as he sat high above the neighborhood.

That was the place to read.

It had not taken Bingo long to climb up to the favorite limb of his youth. He could almost have stepped up onto it. For a moment he could not believe he was on the correct limb. His feet had actually touched the ground.

How long ago had he sat here? Four years? Five? The tree could not have shrunk. He must have grown!

He had sat for a moment, enjoying the awkwardness. It was like being in a booster chair when—

"Hey, Worm Brain!"

Bingo had looked across the yard. It was Wentworth, of course.

"What you doing—playing Tarzan?"

"I've got to read this book." Bingo had given a helpless shrug, gesturing with the closed book as he stepped down from the tree limb.

"What's it about?"

"War."

"War?"

"Yes."

Wentworth had looked interested. "Nam or Gulf?"

"Civil."

"Civil? Hey, let me see that book. Are there any pictures?"

"No."

"Give it here anyway."

And before Bingo knew what was happening, Wentworth was reading aloud and he, Bingo, was lying there on the grass, listening to him.

"That's the end of the dialogue for a while," Wentworth was saying. "I'm glad about that, aren't you?"

"Yes."

"I don't see how actors stand it. I could never be an actor."

"No."

Wentworth picked up the narrative. " 'A shell, screaming like a—' " Wentworth paused to sound out a word. "Ban-shee. Who ever heard of a ban-shee? I swear that's what it says. You can look if you don't believe me."

"I believe you."

"What will they come up with next. '—screaming like a banshee went over the huddled heads of the reserves. It landed in the—' "

Suddenly Wentworth stopped reading. Bingo waited, thinking he was getting ready to sound out a word, but he heard the sound of the book being slammed shut.

"Hey, I almost forgot what I came over for," Wentworth said. "Am I getting stupid or what?" He slapped the side of his head as if to activate his brain.

Bingo didn't answer. He had pushed his new glasses up on his forehead, but now he pulled them down and looked at Wentworth. Wentworth didn't look much better, but Bingo liked to have an excuse—however feeble—to push his glasses up and down.

"I came in the house," Wentworth began, "and my sister said, 'A girl called and wants you to call her back. Her number's by the phone.'

"I look at the number and I recognize it as the Weez's. See, I been dialing Weezie's number lately—I don't know why—every time I pass the phone, I dial the Weez. I hang up as soon as anybody answers, so nobody knows it's me, but I'm beginning to wonder why I do it. I don't want to talk to her. I just want to dial her number. I'm getting so I don't like to pass the phone anymore.

"Anyway, I recognize the number and I dial it. And, Bingo, it takes all my strength not to hang up when some-one answers. I was proud of myself."

Bingo continued to watch Wentworth, though his eyes closed from time to time, as if he were watching bad tele-vision.

"So I don't get Weez. I get Shirl—that's Melissa's sister. Shirl wants to talk. She says, 'You were over here the other day, weren't you?'

"I said, 'Maybe.' I don't give anything away for free.

"She said, 'Were you the big one in camouflage or the one with freckles?'

"I said, 'Do I sound like the one with freckles?'

"She said, 'No.'

"I said, 'Well, I didn't dial this number to be in-sulted.'

"She said, 'Why did you dial it?'

"I said, 'The Weez wanted me to.' That ends the con-versation. She yells, 'Weeee-zie!' Weezie comes to the phone.

"Weezie is naturally jealous that I've been talking to Shirl, but finally she comes out with the reason for the call."

"What was the reason for the call?"

"Melissa's coming over."

Bingo's eyes unglazed.

"Over here?" Bingo went up on one elbow.

"Yeah."

"What did she tell you—exactly?"

"She said, 'Do you think Bingo's home?'"

"I said, 'Who wants to know?' I don't give anything away for free.

"She said, 'Melissa.'

"I said, 'Melissa?'—like I couldn't believe what I was hearing.

"She said, 'Yes, Melissa.'

"I said, 'Well, excuse me, but last time we saw Melissa she ran past Bingo without speaking. Time before that, she didn't give him but seven or eight words. She don't act like somebody who wants to know whether he's home or not. What's she got in mind, Weez—ringing his doorbell and hiding in the bushes?'"

Bingo interrupted. "Wentworth, let me get this straight. Melissa is coming over to my house?"

"You got it."

"This afternoon?" Bingo sat up.

"Yeah." Wentworth checked his watch. "She ought to be here any minute now. I mean, this conversation took place a half-hour ago—maybe more. I lose track of time when I'm reading."

Bingo got to his feet.

"Good-bye, Wentworth."

"You don't mind if I finish this book, do you? It's getting good."

"Be my guest."

"I might even read the hull thing. Get it? Hull thing!"

"Got it," Bingo said as he ran for the house.

The Brown Crisis

Bingo went in the back door just as his mother was attempting to come out of it.

"Bingo, watch what you're doing!"

"Sorry."

He passed her and headed at once for the bathroom. He knew there wouldn't be any mousse, but a quick shave would give him the manly feeling that he needed to meet this new crisis.

"Bingo, wait!"

"I can't! I'm in a hurry."

"I have wonderful news."

"Later."

He rushed into the bathroom and closed the door. He turned on the water so that the drone of his father's electric razor would be muted.

He slid his glasses up on top of his head. He paused. He liked himself almost as much with his glasses on his head as with them on his face. Actually, he would have liked to have two pairs—one for his head and one—

He broke off his thoughts and reached for the razor.

His mother's voice came from just outside the door. She had followed him. Couldn't she leave him alone for one moment without trying to disturb him with wonderful news? Wonderful news was the last thing he wanted to hear when he had to get ready for a mixed-sex conversation.

"The wonderful news is that your father is back to normal!"

"That's nice."

Bingo's hands were trembling with excitement. He fumbled the razor and dropped it. He picked it up by the cord, clicked it on, and took immediate comfort in the normalcy of the buzz. He hadn't broken it.

"I don't know how it happened. I left and he was lying on the bed with his eyes closed to the world, and I come back and he's playing with Jamie. A miracle!"

Bingo began to go over his left cheek.

"And your dad and I are going out!"

"That's nice."

"You look after Jamie."

Bingo was so astonished that he flung open the door without concealing his father's razor. His glasses flopped down onto his face.

"Mom, I can't baby-sit."

"I know. I know." She held up her hands as if in defense. "I said you could have the afternoon to read your book, but Bingo, that was before your father got back to normal!"

"I can't baby-sit."

"Bingo, we want to celebrate. We want to go out and do something fun—have a picnic or bowl or do something we haven't done in years. Go out to the lake and walk barefoot through the sands of time."

"I cannot baby-sit."

"Bingo, you aren't hearing me. Your father is back to normal."

"I hear you fine. *You* are the one who is not hearing me. I cannot baby-sit."

"Why?"

"I have plans."

"What plans?"

"I might—I have reason to believe that I definitely will—have company."

"Company?"

"Yes. Company."

"You can have company. Who, Wentworth? Wentworth won't mind Jamie. Anyway, Wentworth's not company. He's over here all the time."

"This is someone who is not over here 'all the time.' "

"Who?"

"Melissa."

At that moment Bingo's father came from the bedroom. He gave Bingo a smile even when he heard the drone of his razor in Bingo's clenched fist.

His mother backed away from Bingo and turned with a gesture of helplessness to her husband. "He says he's having company."

Bingo shrugged. "Melissa."

"I'm sick of Melissa. I'm fed up with Melissa," his mother hissed. Melissa was a good name to hiss, and his mother gave the name more *s*'s than necessary.

"Now, now," his father said soothingly.

"I can't help it. That girl is just ruining my life. You probably don't remember this, but I almost had a terrible wreck going down Monroe the wrong way. All because of Melissa! And there's another thing I didn't tell you. Remember all those long-distance calls Bingo made to her in Bixby, Oklahoma? He's never completely paid that back. And—"

"Now, now," his father said. "We can work this out."

"How?" his mother asked.

"Let's bend our rules."

"How?"

"Bingo can have company this once without our being home. Melissa can come over and Jamie can be the chaperone."

"Dad, I can't baby-sit. I can't be sitting here with a baby when Melissa comes over. Dad! Be reasonable!"

Bingo's words to his father—that last "Be reasonable!"—were a man-to-man appeal.

After all, his father had once loved a woman. He knew what it was like. He knew that Bingo needed to stand alone, babyless. His hope died when his father gave his that's-the-best-I-can-do shrug.

"All right, we won't go," Bingo's mom said. "We'll all just sit in the living room together. We'll all visit with Melissa."

"I'll baby-sit," Bingo said.

"I don't want to force you," his mother said. "I respect your right not to baby-sit when it interferes with your plans."

"I want to baby-sit."

This caused his mother's frozen features to soften into a smile. "Bingo," she said warmly.

Bingo turned to go back into the bathroom.

"Oh, Bingo," his father said.

"Yes?"

He had a brief moment of hope that his father would give him a wink and say, "We'll take Jamie with us, all right?"

"Yes, Dad?"

"Put my razor back when you're through with it."

"Yes, Dad."

Waiting for Melissa

Bingo sat on the sofa with Jamie on his lap. They were watching cartoons. The Saturday faces were as familiar and comforting to Bingo as his own, and yet now everything the characters did made him nervous.

Also, he had to keep getting up, walking tensely to the window, and looking out. Bingo had been doing this for one hour, and still Melissa had not appeared.

He lowered his new glasses and peered over them like an old man.

"Not yet," he commented. "I wonder where she could be. Maybe she's not coming."

He returned to the sofa and began a sort of nervous commentary about the cartoons.

"Now this is one of my favorites."

He barely knew what he was watching.

"Oh!" At last there was a moment of real recognition. "It *is* one of my favorites. See, that's Wile E. Coyote and he's sending off for a flying machine because he wants to drop a bomb on Road Runner. Road Runner's the one you like so much that goes 'beep-beep.' Don't put your fingers in my mouth, please, Jamie. I'm very nervous. Thank you."

Bingo got up and went to the window. Again, the sidewalk was empty; the street, deserted. It was like the street in a Western movie before the showdown, when townsfolk stayed home behind locked doors.

"Not yet," Bingo said. "I wonder where she can be. Wentworth said she was coming." He paused. "He could have been lying. He could have just said she was coming so that I would run in the house like a fool, shave, put you in a clean jumpsuit, and spend the rest of the afternoon running to the window." He sighed. "But—so far—Wentworth has been truthful—almost too truthful."

He went back to the sofa.

"Now, where were we? Ah, the package has arrived from the Acme Supply Company and, look, Jamie, it turns out to be a flying machine. See, now he's on the flying machine. He gets on the flying machine, and he's supposed to be looking for Road Runner, but he starts enjoying the flying machine and he—"

Ding-dong.

Bingo gasped. His heart leapt to his throat.

It couldn't be Melissa. Already! He hadn't heard her come up the steps. How had she slipped up on him? Had she been hiding in the bushes?

It wasn't fair. He needed time to get himself composed. His plan had been that as soon as he saw her coming down the street, he would compose himself.

Now she was here and there wasn't time to put the plan to work.

Ding-dong.

Bingo leaned forward so he could look out the window and see who was at the door. Perhaps a miracle had occurred and a delivery man . . .

It was Melissa.

Involuntarily, Bingo's arms tightened around his brother.

Melissa was not aware that she was being watched. She fluffed out her hair and put her hands in her pockets and took them out and straightened her collar and put them back and took them out and smoothed her hair. Then she thought better of it and refluffed it.

Ding-dong. Ding-dong.

Two of them! This meant that she was getting tired of the single *ding-dongs* and soon she would tire of the double ones. Then she would come to the window, peer in to see if anybody was home. And she would see him, frozen with fear on the sofa.

Bingo got up at once and started for the door. He held

Jamie in both arms. This way he didn't have to worry about an embrace. An embrace could obviously not be accomplished without dropping or crushing or in some way endangering his brother's health.

"Coming!" he called, feigning nonchalance. He was grateful for Jamie. Anyone facing a perilous situation—and Bingo considered himself an expert on those—should hold a baby. They made wonderful shields.

He reached around Jamie and opened the door.

"Oh, Bingo!" Melissa said. "Your brother!"

"Yes."

"He looks just like you!"

"Really?"

"He's just darling!"

"Thanks."

"And he's got freckles! You didn't say he had freckles. Those little spots are freckles, aren't they?"

"We're hoping."

"And Bingo!"

"What? What?"

"You've got glasses."

"Yes."

"I know you didn't get glasses so you'd look sexy, but . . . but you do."

"Oh, really?"

"Yes."

"I thought they made me look . . . a little studious."

She looked at him a moment, studying him closely. "That, too."

"Sexy and studious?"

"Yes."

There was a silence. Bingo couldn't speak. If he could have gone through the entire dictionary and chosen any two adjectives out of all the adjectives in the entire world to describe himself, those were the two he would have chosen.

He should have gotten those glasses years ago. He should have gotten them in nursery school. But then if he had had them all along, his appearance would have been taken for granted, while—

Melissa cleared her throat. "Is it all right if I come in?"

"Oh, yes, of course."

She glanced both ways before entering, as if his living room were a busy intersection. "Your parents aren't here?"

"No, they're off celebrating my father's return to being normal."

"I wish my father would do that," Melissa said wistfully. "He hasn't been normal since he lost his first job, and that was over a year ago."

They crossed the living room and sat together on the sofa. The sofa wasn't used to being sat on by two people at the exact same time and gave a surprised *whoosh*.

Bingo pressed the mute button on the TV remote control, and a silence filled the living room.

Melissa reached out and took Jamie's hand. She held it absently. Then she looked directly into Bingo's eyes.

She sighed.

And there was something about that sigh that let Bingo know Melissa was getting ready to say something that would change his life forever.

The Best Mixed-Sex Conversation in the History of the World

Bingo waited, his heart pumping anxiously against his brother's jumpsuit.

"I came to say good-bye," Melissa said.

These were the last words Bingo wanted to hear. He asked, "Good-bye?" and then gave his own answer. "You're saying good-bye."

She glanced down and nodded. When she looked up, her eyelashes were wet.

Bingo had never looked into eyes framed in wet eyelashes, and he was deeply affected. He blinked to keep his own eyelashes dry.

"Then you aren't back to stay?"

"No."

"I didn't know. Nobody told me. I just hoped."

"I did, too. We were going to stay with my cousin

Weezie while Dad looked for a job. I was really looking forward to it—being back here, seeing all my friends . . . seeing you."

She shook her head and her hair fanned out about her face. "But it wouldn't have worked anyway."

"Why, Melissa? Why?"

"Oh, at first it was fun. It was like being in a dormitory. And then little things started happening, like Shirl used Brenda's fingernail polish and didn't put the top back on. And Libby used up all the hot water and Bettie had to shampoo with cold. And Weezie claimed I ruined her hair. I didn't ruin it. Half of it was perfect. You saw it!"

Bingo nodded.

"Anyway, it was just one thing after another, Bingo."

Bingo nodded sympathetically. "Life's like that sometimes."

"Anyway, my dad's found a job—of sorts—in a muffler shop in Pickens, South Carolina. He doesn't want to go to Pickens, and I don't either. Neither does my mom— she calls it Slim Pickens—but we're going."

"Pickens will be better with you in it."

"Oh, thank you." She swallowed. Even her gulp had a beautiful sound.

"I hope you can forgive me, Bingo."

"Of course," he said quickly. As usual, he had spoken too quickly. "For what?"

"For acting so funny."

"I act funny myself at times," Bingo admitted. He

continued in a rush. "Like, I write a letter and mail the Xerox of the letter, and nobody—least of all somebody in love—would do that except out of stupidity."

"Or out of too much emotion."

Bingo felt a flush of gratitude. "I certainly have that."

"And when I get emotional—I can't explain it, but that's the way I was in the grocery store, and I don't know, I mean, well, you didn't look like I remembered. You looked older."

"Older?" This was one of the best mixed-sex conversations in the history of the world. There was not a word in it that wasn't perfect. Bingo would have liked to have a tape of it, even though it would play in his memory forever.

"And, I don't know, I just couldn't speak. I'm not explaining this very well."

"You are. You are! I couldn't speak either."

"Really, Bingo?"

"Yes."

She smiled, and he thought of an old-timey phrase he had read in a book once: "She smiled through her tears." His heart ached.

Bingo held his brother tighter when he saw her small, pointed teeth. "You always say the right thing to me."

"I try."

"Bingo, can I ask you a favor?"

"Of course."

"Would you keep on writing me letters?"

"I wasn't sure you liked them."

"I do. I love them. I don't even care if they're Xeroxes!"

"They won't be."

"And I don't know, I just feel like if I thought, well, I was never going to get another one of your letters, it would make me even sadder than I am."

"I wouldn't want that to happen."

"Then you will write?"

"Yes."

"But just . . . just . . . friendly stuff."

Bingo understood that there would be no more talk of the hunger of love, no matter how loudly his stomach rumbled.

"I'll try to write about what I'm doing and what's going on around here, things like that," he said manfully.

"Thank you, Bingo."

"You're welcome."

She stood up. "I have to go."

"Already?"

She was still holding Jamie's hand. It was awkward to stand without breaking the connection, but Bingo managed it.

She didn't seem to want to let go. Bingo didn't want her to let go either. He didn't want her to go—period. It was as if she was taking something of great value with her, something that might never come again.

She sighed.

Bingo resorted to a desperate half-truth. He said, "Jamie can say bye-bye." It wasn't what he wanted to say, but he had to keep her from leaving. Her face brightened, which made the half-truth worthwhile.

"Really?"

"Well, he can say it, but he doesn't know when to say it."

She leaned forward over Jamie's small hand. "Bye-bye, Jamie, bye-bye," she said, looking into his round eyes. "Will you tell me good-bye? Next time I see you, you might be a great big boy. Bye-bye."

Bingo didn't dare to hope. "Sometimes he won't say it—and then sometimes he says it when it's not appropriate—like in the bathtub and—"

Jamie came through. "Bye-bye-bye-bye-bye," he said. Five of them! Well, two and a half.

Bingo thought he would burst with emotion—with pride and sorrow and loss.

"Good-bye, Jamie," Melissa said in the kindest voice Bingo had ever heard. Then she looked at him, and in the same kind way she said, "Good-bye, Bingo."

She took one step forward and pressed her lips to his. It was so unexpected that Bingo didn't have time to get his lips ready.

She pulled back and eyed him. "Bingo Brown, have you been kissing other girls?"

"No. No!" He was pleased he did not blurt out that he hadn't even been trying. "Why?"

"Because you kiss better."

"Better?"

Bingo wanted to ask her to repeat that, but instead he smiled and said coolly, "Well, you know, when you've got it . . ."

Melissa grinned. Then she swirled. Her hair fanned out, leaving the faint scent of gingersnaps in the room. Then she went out the door.

Bingo continued to stand in the open door with Jamie in his arms, watching until she was out of sight. He felt both better and worse than he had ever felt in his life.

After the Last Cartoon

Bingo started back to the sofa. "That was Melissa—the girl you've heard so much about," he told the back of Jamie's neck.

Somewhere a phone rang.

"And you don't know this, but you have just heard a mixed-sex conversation so great it could go down in the history of mixed-sex conversations."

The phone rang again. Bingo looked up, surprised. "Oh, that's our phone." He shifted Jamie to his hip and picked up the phone.

"Bingo, hi, it's me—Mom."

"Hi."

"You getting along all right?"

"Fine."

"Did Melissa come?"

"She came . . . and went."

"I hope Jamie didn't, well, inhibit you."

"Not at all."

"Good. I tell you why I called. You're going to think this is silly, but I made Jamie some Jell-O."

"What?"

"I made Jell-O, and I want to see Jamie get his first bite, because I remember how cute you were. You got this little expression—well, I couldn't even describe it—it was hopeful and puzzled and—it was like you'd just gotten proof that the world was going to be full of good little surprises."

"Actually, it is."

"Anyway, I was afraid you'd see the Jell-O and give it to him for lunch."

"I probably would have."

"So you'll wait?"

"Yes." He hung up the phone and carried Jamie back to the sofa.

He picked up the TV remote control, but he didn't turn on the sound. He began to speak to his brother.

"You know how Mom's always writing in your baby book? First word, first tooth, first Jell-O. Well, Jamie, that was my first love."

The thought made Bingo draw a deep, trembling breath.

"As first loves go," he continued when he could speak, "I would have to give it a ten. It was a love for all time, for eternity, maybe even infinity, and I guess it doesn't get any better than that."

"Bye-bye," Jamie said. Bingo wondered if he would ever hear a baby's bye-bye without remembering this moment.

Bingo sighed.

"Oh, this is the last cartoon. It's Porky Pig and, Jamie, when he says, 'Th-that's all, folks,' we'll go in the kitchen and I'll fix your bottle. It's time for your nap."

Bingo turned on the sound. He sat without speaking during the cartoon.

He was filled with memories. He thought of the day in English class when he had fallen in love with Melissa. He thought of their many mixed-sex conversations, of their kiss that day on her front porch in the rain. He thought of their exchange of gifts—he still had his notebook holder, and she— He broke off to think. Had she had on the gypsy earrings he had given her? He thought so. In his memory she had. Then, of course, he thought of their parting.

He took a deep breath. He remembered a line from *The Red Badge of Courage*.

"He felt a quiet manhood, not assertive, but of sturdy and strong blood."

He exhaled, breathed in again. He remembered another line.

"He turned with a lover's thirst to images of tranquil skies, fresh meadows, cool brooks—an existence of soft and eternal peace."

And as he took one more of these deep breaths, Bingo found he was filled not only with air and quiet manhood, but a firm resolve.

He had thought to discontinue his *Guide to Romance* because of a lack of knowledge of the subject. He would not let that deter him now. He saw how words—even words written over a hundred years ago—could bring comfort. And how much more comfort would there be in words written by a brother?

Problem #9. Maintaining a Quiet Manhood.

The TV intruded into these pleasant thoughts. Bingo heard, "Th-that's all, folks."

He got up at once. He always kept his word to his baby brother. "I can't give you any Jell-O—I promised— but there's this noise that Jell-O makes when you dig out the first spoonful—and I can go ahead and show you the sound . . ."

And Bingo Brown and his baby brother disappeared into the kitchen.